SKY'S STORIES

Written by: Heddrick McBride

Illustrated by: HH-Pax

Edited by: Tilea Coleman and Jean P. Gaillard

Copyright © 2012 Heddrick M. McBride

All rights reserved.

ISBN: 1481112201

ISBN-13:978-148111208

Hello my name is Skylar, but my friends call me Sky.

Let me tell you about myself. I will give it a try.

I love to play outside, but I also love school.

I think reading books and playing sports is cool.

I listen to my parents because they know what is best.

I eat vegetables, drink water, and get plenty of rest.

I love family, friends, and fun. Just to name a few.

I will share some of my stories with you.

A Trip to the Zoo

We went to the zoo; just my Daddy and me.

Let me tell you about the animals that we would see.

The giraffes were standing tall and proud, as peaceful as can be.

How amazing that their necks could reach the top of the tree.

There were also bears in the field, as plain as day.

It looked like a lot of fun, the way that they played.

We looked at all the zebras covered with black and white.

Wow, that was a very special sight.

How cute were those monkeys? They were all over the place.

I couldn't stop laughing at their cute little faces.

I thanked my Daddy for taking me on a trip to the zoo.

He smiled and told me that he had fun too.

A Party for a Princess

Of all the birthday parties I had, this year was the best.

My Daddy called it a party for a princess.

Of course my Mommy and Daddy were there.
They threw me this party because they care.

Also having fun with me were many of my friends.
We danced and played games from the beginning to the end.

My parents bought me a big beautiful birthday cake.
I would have eaten the whole thing until I had a tummy ache.

My Daddy held the piñata that was full of candy and treats.

Once it was broken the kids knew that they could eat.

I opened all of my gifts, and then went home to get some rest.

I was very tired after having a party for a princess.

Candy Day

This year's Halloween was the best, I must say.

From now on we will call it *Candy Day*.

Elizabeth had whiskers with her cat costume.
Vanessa was the wicked witch, she even had a broom.

Ryan was a skeleton that showed all of his bones.

He already had candy, because he went to four homes.

My Daddy and I were a nice sight to see.

I was a beautiful elf, and he was dressed like me.

We all went home and said goodnight.
Bags full of candy were a beautiful sight.

Mommy vs. Daddy

I love my Mommy and my Daddy, but who is the best?

I had to put them through a test.

Mommy is the one who gives me bubble baths
Daddy does funny things that make me laugh.

When I am sick, my Mommy rubs my head.

My Daddy reads me stories and tucks me into bed.

Daddy brought home a large Christmas tree.

Mommy decorated it with lights, so that everyone could see.

Mommy taught me manners and to treat people right.

Daddy showed me how to work hard every day and night.

Mommy runs with me; she brings me to the track.

Daddy taught me how to catch a ball and to throw it back.

Mommy showed me how to dance. She has good moves.

Daddy taught me to take my time and be smooth.

They both taught me about love, family and giving.

They both talk about school, sports and healthy living.

After counting all of the scores, my decision has been made.

Mommy and Daddy both earned the exact same grade.

They both give me everything, much more than the rest.

I guess that is why together they are the best.

Family Day at the Park

The sun was shining brightly. It was a beautiful day.

Mommy and Daddy took me outside to play.

It was "Family Day;" we all went to the park.

We had so much fun before it got dark.

Where do I start? We did so many things.

The first thing I did was play on the swings.

I was thirsty, so I got some water from the fountain.
Those sliding boards reminded me of climbing a mountain.

On this long day, my favorite part of it all;

I watched my Daddy playing basketball.

We were lucky enough to have one more treat.

The ice cream from the truck that was right up the street.

VISIT
WWW.MCBRIDESTORIES.COM
FOR MORE TITLES

Made in the USA
Middletown, DE
03 October 2024